THE
FATHER
CHRISTMAS
LETTERS

J. R. R. TOLKIEN

THE FATHER CHRISTMAS LETTERS

Edited by Baillie Tolkien

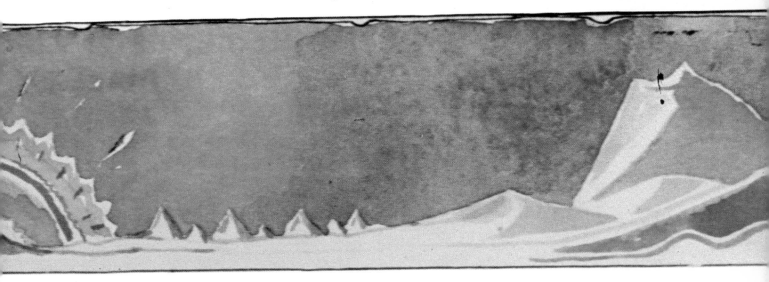

London

George Allen & Unwin Ltd

RUSKIN HOUSE · MUSEUM STREET

Cliff House
near the North Pole.
✳ December 21st ✳
1933.

My dears

Another Christmas! and I almost thought at one time (in November) that there would not be one this year. There would be the 25th of Dec. of course, but nothing from your old great-great-great-etc. grandfather at the North Pole. My pictures tell you part of the story. **Goblins.** The worst attack we have had for centuries. They have been fearfully wild and angry ever since we took all their stolen toys off them last year & dosed them with green smoke. You remember the Red Gnomes promised to clear all of them out. There was not one to be found in any hole or cave by New Years day. But I said they would crop up again – in a century or so. They have not waited so long! They must have gathered their nasty friends from mountains all over the world, & been busy all the summer while we were at our sleepiest. This time we had very little warning. Soon after All Saints' Day PB got very restless. He now says he smelt nasty smells — but as usual he did not say anything; he says he did not want to trouble me. He really is a nice old thing, & this time he absolutely saved Christmas. He took to sleeping in the kitchen with his nose towards the cellar-door, opening on the main-stairway down into my big stores.

One night just about Christopher's birthday, I woke up suddenly. The fire was squeaking and spluttering in the room & a nasty smell — in my own best green & purple room that I had

INTRODUCTION

To the children of J. R. R. Tolkien, the interest and importance of Father Christmas extended beyond his filling of their stockings on Christmas Eve; for he wrote a letter to them every year, in which he described in words and pictures his house, and his friends, and the events, hilarious or alarming, at the North Pole. The first of the letters came in 1920, when John, the eldest, was three years old; and for over twenty years, through the childhoods of the three other children, Michael, Christopher and Priscilla, they continued to arrive each Christmas. Sometimes the envelopes, dusted with snow and bearing Polar postage stamps, were found in the house on the morning after his visit; sometimes the postman brought them; and letters that the children wrote themselves vanished from the fireplace when no one was about.

As time went on, Father Christmas' household became larger, and whereas

at first little is heard of anyone else except the North Polar Bear, later on there appear Snow-elves, Red Gnomes, Snow-men, Cave-bears, and the Polar Bear's nephews, Paksu and Valkotukka, who came on a visit and never went away. But the Polar Bear remained Father Christmas' chief assistant, and the chief cause of the disasters that led to muddles and deficiencies in the Christmas stockings; and sometimes he wrote on the letters his comments in angular capitals.

Eventually Father Christmas took on as his secretary an Elf named Ilbereth,

Christmas House
NORTH POLE
1920

LOVE to
daddy, mummy
michael & aunt .2
& mary

Dear John,
I heard you ask daddy
what I was like & where
I lived. I have drawn
ME & My House for you.
Take care of the picture.
I am just off now for
Oxford with my bundle
of toys — some for you.
Hope I shall arrive in
time: the snow is very
thick at the NORTH POLE
tonight. yr loving Fr. Chr.

FROM FATHER ○ CHRISTMAS

ME

FC

MY HOUSE

FC

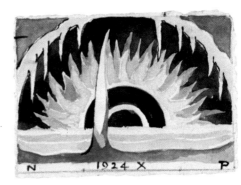

and in the later letters Elves play an important part in the defence of Father Christmas' house and store-cellars against attacks by Goblins.

In this book it has been possible to give only a few examples of Father Christmas' shaky handwriting, and of the decorations of the letters and the envelopes. But almost all the pictures that he sent are here reproduced; and at the end is given the alphabet that the Polar Bear devised from the Goblin drawings on the walls of the caves where he was lost, and the letter that he sent to the children written in it.

You have been so good in writing to me (& such beautiful letters too), that I have tried to draw you some specially nice pictures this year. At the top of my 'Christmas card' is a picture, imaginary, but more or less as it really is, of me arriving over Oxford. Your house is just about where the three little black points stick up out of the shadows at the right. I am coming from the north you see — & note NOT with 12 pair of deer, as you will see in some books. I usually use 7 pair (14 is such a nice number), & at Christmas, especially if I am hurried, I add my 2 special white ones in front.

1925

I am dreadfully busy this year – it makes my hand more shaky than ever when I think of it – and not very rich. In fact, awful things have been happening, and some of the presents have got spoilt and I haven't got the North Polar Bear to help me and I have had to move house just before Christmas, so you can imagine what a state everything is in, and you will see why I have a new address. It all happened like this: one very windy day last November my hood blew off and went and stuck on the top of the North Pole. I told him not to, but the North Polar Bear climbed up to the thin top to get it down – and he did. The pole broke in the middle and fell on the roof of my house, and the North Polar Bear fell through the hole it made into the dining room with my hood over his nose, and all the snow fell off the roof into the house and melted and put out all the fires and ran down into the cellars where I was collecting this year's presents, and the North Polar Bear's leg got broken. He is well again now, but I was so cross with him that he says he won't try to help me again. I expect his temper is hurt, and will be mended by next Christmas. I send you a picture of the accident, and of my new house on the cliffs above the North Pole (with beautiful cellars in the cliffs). If John can't read my old shaky writing (1925 years old) he must get his father to. When is Michael going to learn to read, and write his own letters to me? Lots of love to you both and Christopher, whose name is rather like mine.

1925

These stars shot!

this
Star went
red when
Pole snapped

The N.P.Bear
with my
head.
and a bit
of the roof

N.P. broken.

lumps of roof
on floor

Me! angry

my new house

See where we
put up new N.Pole
on the old stump
joined on with
red.

windows of
new cellars

The star gone
yellow again

my reindeer can
climb up the
cliff.

1925

my old house

me! busy

1926

I am more shaky than usual this year. The North Polar Bear's fault! It was the biggest bang in the world, and the most monstrous firework there ever has been. It turned the North Pole BLACK and shook all the stars out of place, broke the moon into four – and the Man in it fell into my back garden. He ate quite a lot of my Christmas chocolates before he said he felt better, and climbed back to mend it and get the stars tidy. Then I found out that the reindeer had broken loose. They were running all over the country, breaking reins and ropes and tossing presents up in the air. They were all packed up to start, you see – yes it only happened this morning; it was a sleighload of chocolate things – which I always send to England early. I hope yours are not badly damaged. But isn't the North Polar Bear silly? And he isn't a bit sorry! Of course he did it – you remember I had to move last year because of him? The tap turning on the Aurora Borealis fireworks is still in the cellar of my old house. The North Polar Bear knew he must never, never touch it. I only let it off on special days like Christmas. He says he thought it was cut off since we moved – anyway he was nosing round the ruins this morning soon after breakfast (he hides things to eat there) and turned on all the Northern Lights for two years in one go. You have never heard or seen anything like it. I have tried to draw a picture of it; but I am too shaky to do it properly and you can't paint fizzing light, can you?

Love from Father Christmas
1926.

1927

It has been so bitter at the North Pole lately that the North Polar Bear has spent most of the time asleep and has been less use than usual this Christmas. The North Pole became colder than any cold thing ever has been, and when the North Polar Bear put his nose against it, it took the skin off: that is why it is bandaged with red flannel in the picture (but the bandage has slipped). Why did he? I don't know, but he is always putting his nose where it oughtn't to be – into my cupboards, for instance.

Also it has been very dark here since winter began. We haven't seen the Sun, of course, for three months, and there are no Northern Lights this year – you remember the awful accident last year? There will be none again until the end of 1928. The North Polar Bear has got his cousin (and distant friend), the GREAT BEAR, to shine extra bright for us, and this week I have hired a comet to do my packing by, but it doesn't work as well – you can see that by my picture. The North Polar Bear has not really been any more sensible this year: yesterday he was snowballing the Snow-man in the garden and pushed him over the edge of the cliff so that he fell into my sleigh at the bottom and broke lots of things – one of them was himself. I used some of what was left of him to paint my white picture.

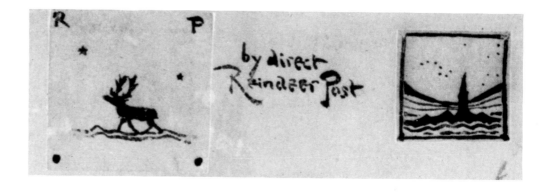

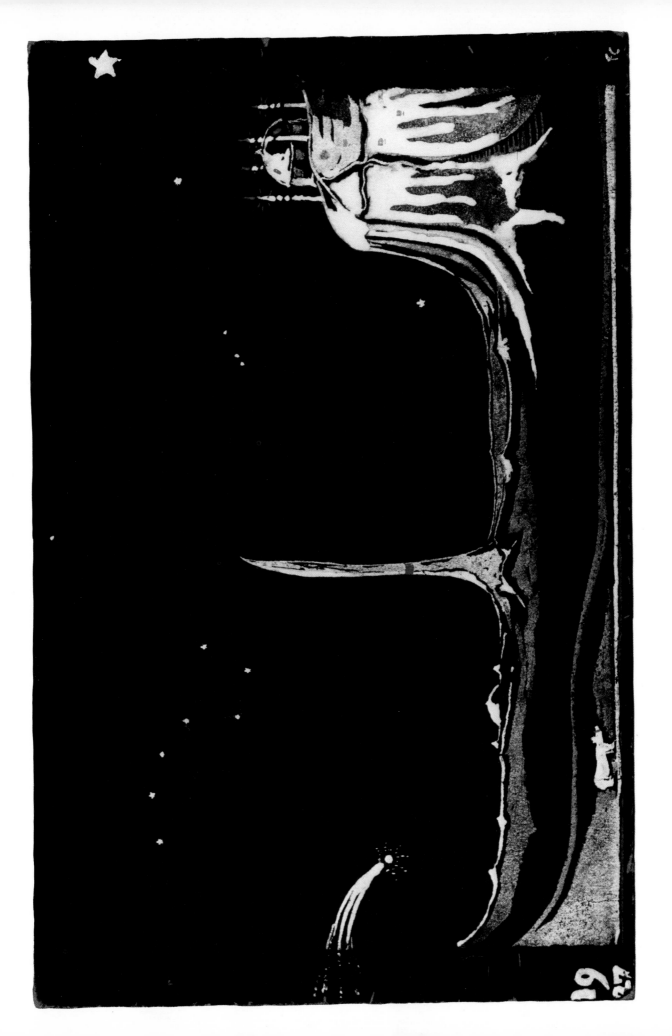

1928

What do you think the poor dear old bear has been and done this time? Nothing as bad as letting off all the lights. Only fell from top to bottom of the main stairs on Thursday! We were beginning to get the first lot of parcels down out of the store-rooms into the hall. Polar Bear would insist on taking an enormous pile on his head as well as lots in his arms. Bang Rumble Clatter Crash! awful moanings and growlings: I ran out onto the landing and saw he had fallen from top to bottom onto his nose leaving a trail of balls bundles parcels and things all the way down – and he had fallen on top of some and smashed them. I hope you got none of these by accident? I have drawn you a picture of it all. Polar Bear was rather grumpy at my drawing it: he says my Christmas pictures always make fun of him and that one year he will send one drawn by himself of me being idiotic (but of course I never am, and he can't draw well enough). When he had picked himself up he ran out of doors and wouldn't help clear up because I sat on the stairs and laughed as soon as I found there was not much damage done.

But anyway I thought you would like a picture of the INSIDE of my new big house for a change. This is the chief hall under the largest dome where we pile the presents usually, ready to load on the sleighs at the doors. Polar Bear and I built it nearly all ourselves, and laid all the blue and mauve tiles. The banisters and roof are not quite straight, but it doesn't really matter. I painted the pictures on the walls of the trees and stars and suns and moons.

"Top o' the World"
NORTH POLE
Thursday December 20th
1928

1929

It is a light Christmas again, I am glad to say – the Northern Lights have been specially good. We had a bonfire this year (to please the Polar Bear), to celebrate the coming in of winter. The Snow-elves let off all the rockets together which surprised us both. I have tried to draw you a picture of it, but really there were hundreds of rockets. You can't see the Elves at all against the snow background. The bonfire made a hole in the ice and woke up the Great Seal, who happened to be underneath. The Polar Bear let off 20,000 silver sparklers afterwards – used up all my stock, so that is why I had none to send you. Then he went for a holiday!!! – to north Norway – and stayed with a wood-cutter called Olaf, and came back with his paw all bandaged just at the beginning of our busy times.

There seem more children than ever in all the countries I specially look after. It is a good thing clocks don't tell the same time all over the world or I should never get round, although when my magic is strongest – at Christmas – I can do about a thousand stockings a minute, if I have it all planned out beforehand. You could hardly guess the enormous piles of lists I make out. I seldom get them mixed. But I am rather worried this year. You can guess from my pictures what happened. The first one shows you my office and packing room and the Polar Bear reading out names while I copy them down. We had awful gales here, worse than you did, tearing clouds of snow to a million tatters, screaming like demons, burying my house almost up to the roofs. Just at the worst the Polar Bear said it was stuffy! and opened a north window before I could stop him. Look at the result – only actually the North Polar Bear was buried in papers and lists; but that did not stop him laughing.

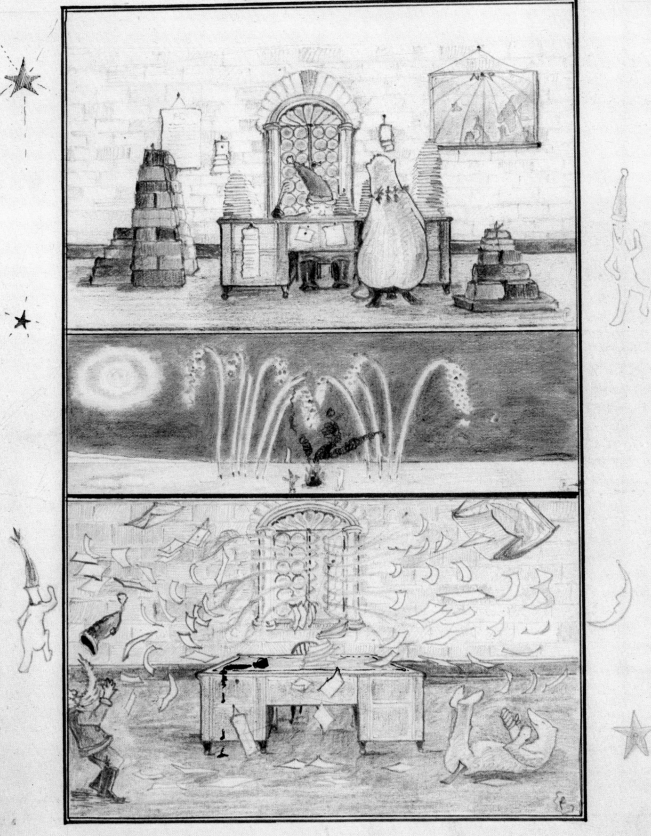

1930

I have enjoyed all your letters: I hope you will like your stockings this year: I tried to find what you asked for, but the stores have been in rather a muddle – you see the Polar Bear has been ill. He had whooping-cough first of all. I could not let him help with the packing and sorting which begins in November – because it would be simply awful if any of my children caught Polar Whooping Cough and barked like bears on Boxing Day. So I had to do everything myself in the preparations. Of course Polar Bear has done his best – he cleaned up and mended my sleigh and looked after the reindeer while I was busy. That is how the really bad accident happened. Early this month we had a most awful snow-storm (nearly six feet of snow) followed by an awful fog. The poor Polar Bear went out to the reindeer stables and got lost and nearly buried. I did not miss him or go to look for him for a long while. His chest had not got well from Whooping Cough so this made him frightfully ill, and he was in bed until three days ago. Everything has gone wrong and there has been no one to look after my messengers properly.

Aren't you glad the Polar Bear is better? We had a party of Snow-boys (sons of the Snow-men, which are the only sort of people that live near – not of course men *made* of snow, though my gardener who is the oldest of all the Snow-men sometimes draws a picture of a *made* Snow-man instead of writing his name) and Polar Cubs (the Polar Bear's nephews) on Saturday, as soon as he felt well enough. He didn't eat much tea, but when the big cracker went off after, he threw away his rug, and leaped in the air, and has been well ever since.

The top picture shows Polar Bear telling a story after all the things had been cleared away. The little pictures show me finding Polar Bear in the snow, and Polar Bear sitting with his feet in hot mustard and water to stop him shivering. It didn't – and he sneezed so terribly he blew five candles out. Still, he is all right now – I know because he has been at his tricks again: quarrelling with the Snow-man (my gardener) and pushing him through the roof of his snow house;

and packing lumps of ice instead of presents in naughty children's parcels. That might be a good idea only he never told me and some of them (with ice) were put in warm store-rooms and melted all over good children's presents!

Well, my dears, there is lots more I should like to say – about my Green Brother, and my father, old Grandfather Yule, and why we were both called Nicholas after the Saint (whose day is December sixth) who used to give secret presents, sometimes throwing purses of money through the window. But I must hurry away – I am late already and I am afraid you may not get this in time.

1930

Party of Snowboys & Polar-cubs to celebrate P.B.'s recovery.

P.B. recovers!

1931

My latest portrait — Father Christmas packing
1931. Love to you all. Your loving
N.C.

Here is my latest portrait – Father Christmas packing, 1931. If you find that not many of the things you asked for have come, and not perhaps quite so many as sometimes, remember that this Christmas all over the world there are a terrible number of poor and starving people. I (and also my Green Brother) have had to do some collecting of food and clothes, and toys too, for the children whose fathers and mothers cannot give them anything, sometimes not even dinner.

It has gone on being warm up here – not what you would call warm, but warm for the North Pole, with very little snow. The North Polar Bear has been lazy and sleepy as a result, and very slow over packing, or any job except eating – he has enjoyed sampling and tasting the food parcels this year (to see if they were fresh and good, he said). But that is not the worst. I should hardly feel it was Christmas if he didn't do something ridiculous. You will never guess what he did this time! I sent him down into one of my cellars – the cracker-hole, we call it – where I keep thousands of boxes of crackers (you would like to see them, rows upon rows, all with their lids off to show the kinds of colours) – well, I wanted twenty boxes and was busy sorting soldiers and farm things so I sent him; and he was so lazy he took Snow-boys (who aren't allowed down there) to help him. They started pulling crackers out of boxes, and he tried to box them (the boys' ears I mean), and they dodged and he fell over, and let his candle fall right POOF! into my firework-crackers and boxes of sparklers. I could hear the noise and smell the smell in the hall; and when I rushed down I saw nothing but smoke and fizzing stars, and old Polar Bear was rolling over on the floor with sparks sizzling in his coat; he has quite a bare patch burnt on his back. The Snow-boys roared with laughter and then ran away. They said it was a splendid sight, but they won't come to my party on St Stephen's Day; they have had more than their share already.

——This is all drawn by the North Polar Bear. Don't you think he is getting better? But the green ink is mine – and he didn't ask for it.

Two of the Polar Bear's nephews have been staying here for some time – Paksu and Valkotukka ('fat' and 'white-hair' they say it means). They are fat-tummied Polar Cubs and are very funny, boxing one another and rolling about. But another time I shall have them on Boxing Day and not just at packing-time. I fell over them fourteen times a day last week. And Valkotukka swallowed a ball of red string, thinking it was cake, and he got it all wound up inside and had a tangled cough – he couldn't sleep at night, but I thought it rather served him right for putting holly in my bed. It was the same cub that poured all the black

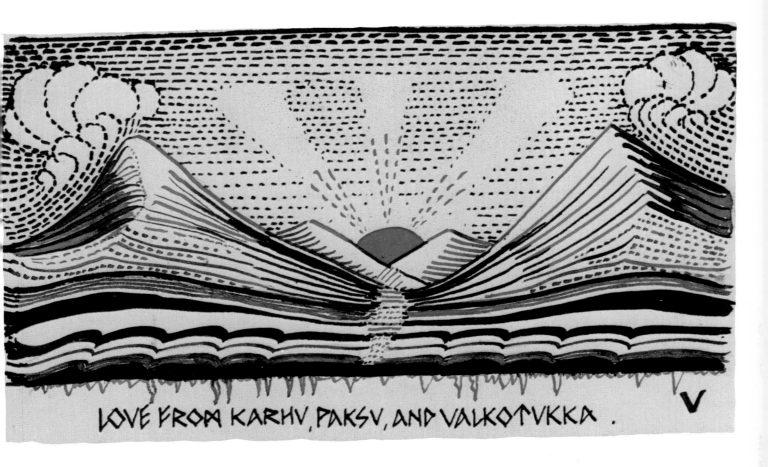

LOVE FROM KARHV, PAKSV, AND VALKOTVKKA .

ink yesterday into the fire – to make night: it did, and a very smelly smoky one. We lost Paksu all last Wednesday and found him on Thursday morning asleep in a cupboard in the kitchen; he had eaten two whole puddings raw. They seem to be growing up just like their uncle.

Goodbye now. I shall soon be off on my travels once more. You need not believe any pictures you see of me in aeroplanes or motors. I cannot drive one, and I don't want to; and they are too slow anyway (not to mention smell), they cannot compare with my own *reindeer*, which I train myself. They are all very well this year, and I expect my posts will be in very good time. I have got some new young ones this Christmas from Lapland.

1932

There have been lots of adventures you will want to hear about. It all began with the funny noises underground which started in the summer and got worse and worse. I was afraid an earthquake might happen. The North Polar Bear says he suspected what was wrong from the beginning. I only wish he had said something to me; and anyway it can't be quite true, as he was fast asleep when it began, and did not wake up till about Michael's birthday.* However, he went off for a walk one day, at the end of November, I think, and never came back! About a fortnight ago I began to be really worried, for after all the dear old thing is really a lot of help, in spite of accidents, and very amusing. One Friday evening (December 9th), there was a bumping at the front door and a snuffling. I thought he had come back, and lost his key (as often before); but when I opened the door there was another very old bear there, a very fat and funny-shaped one. Actually it was the eldest of the few remaining Cave-bears. (I had not seen him for centuries.)

'Do you want your North Polar Bear?' he said. 'If you do, you had better come and get him!'

It turned out he was lost in the caves (belonging to Cave-Bear, or so he says) not far from the ruins of my old house. He says he found a hole in the side of a hill and went inside because it was snowing. He slipped down a long slope, and lots of rock fell after him, and he found he could not climb up or get out again. But almost at once he smelt GOBLIN! and became interested and started to explore. Not very wise, for of course Goblins can't hurt *him*, but their caves are very dangerous. Naturally he soon got quite lost, and the Goblins shut off all their lights, and made queer noises and false echoes.

Goblins are to us very much what rats are to you, only worse, because they are very clever, and only better because there are, in these parts, very few. We thought there were none left. Long ago we had great trouble with them, that was about 1453, I believe, but we got the help of the Gnomes, who are their greatest enemies, and cleared them out. Anyway, there was poor old Polar Bear lost in the dark all among them, and alone until he met Cave-Bear, who lives there. Cave-Bear can see pretty well in the dark, and he offered to take Polar Bear to his private back door. So they set off together, but the Goblins were very excited and angry (Polar Bear had boxed one or two flat that came and poked him in the dark, and had said some very nasty things to them all), and they enticed him away by imitating Cave-Bear's voice, which of course they know very well. So Polar Bear got into a frightful dark part, all full of different passages, and he lost Cave-Bear, and Cave-Bear lost him.

'Light is what we need,' said Cave-Bear to me. So I got some of my special sparkling torches – which I sometimes use in my deepest cellars – and we set off that night. The caves are wonderful. I knew they were there, but not how many or how big they were. Of course the Goblins went off into the deepest holes and

* 22 October

corners, and we soon found Polar Bear. He was getting quite long and thin with hunger, as he had been in the caves about a fortnight. He said, 'I should soon have been able to squeeze through a Goblin crack.'

Polar Bear himself was astonished when I brought light; for the most remarkable thing is that the walls of these caves are all covered with pictures, cut into the rock or painted on in red and brown and black. Some of them are very good (mostly of animals) and some are queer, and some bad, and there are many strange marks, signs and scribbles, some of which have a nasty look, and I am sure have something to do with black magic. Cave-Bear says these caves belong to him, and have belonged to him or his family since the days of his great-great-great-great-great-great-great-great-great-(multiplied by ten) grandfather; and the bears first had the idea of decorating the walls, and used to scratch pictures on them in soft parts – it was useful for sharpening the claws. Then MEN came along – imagine it! Cave-Bear says there were lots about at one time, long ago, when the North Pole was somewhere else. (That was long before my time, and I have never heard old Grandfather Yule mention it, even, so I don't know if he's talking nonsense or not.) Many of the pictures were done by these Cave-men – the best ones, especially the big ones (almost life-size) of animals, some of which have since disappeared: there are *dragons* and quite a lot of mammoths. Men also put some of the black marks and pictures there, but the Goblins have scribbled all over the place. They can't draw well, and anyway they like nasty queer shapes best.

I have copied a whole page from the wall of the chief central cave. It is not, perhaps, quite as well drawn as the originals (which are very much larger) except the Goblin parts, which are easy. At the bottom of the page you will see a whole row of Goblin pictures – they must be very old, because the Goblin fighters are sitting on *drasils*: a very queer sort of dwarf 'dachshund' horse creature they used to use, but they have died out long ago. I believe the Red Gnomes finished them off, somewhere about Edward the Fourth's time. You will see some more on the pillar in my picture of the caves.

Doesn't the hairy rhinoceros look wicked? There is also a nasty look in the mammoth's eyes. You will also see an ox, a stag, a boar, a cave-bear (portrait of our Cave-Bear's seventy-first ancestor, he says) and some other kind of polarish but not quite polar bear. North Polar Bear would like to believe it is a portrait of one of *his* ancestors. Just under the bears you can see what is the best a Goblin can do at drawing reindeer!!!

But when I rescued Polar Bear we hadn't finished the adventures. At the beginning of last week we went into the cellars to get up the stuff for England.

I said to Polar Bear, 'Somebody has been disarranging things here!'

'Paksu and Valkotukka, I expect,' he said. But it wasn't. Then last Saturday we went down and found nearly everything had *disappeared* out of the main cellar! Imagine my state of mind! Nothing hardly to send to anybody, and too

little time to get or make enough new stuff.

Polar Bear said, 'I smell Goblin strong'. Eventually we found a large hole (but not big enough for us) leading to a tunnel, behind some packing-cases in the West Cellar. As you will expect, we rushed off to find Cave-Bear and we went back to the caves. We soon understood the queer noises. It was plain the Goblins long ago had burrowed a tunnel from the caves to my old home (which was not so far from the end of their hills) and had stolen a good many things. We found some things more than a hundred years old, even a few parcels still addressed to your great-grand-people! But they had been very clever, and not too greedy, and I had not found out. Ever since I moved they must have been busy burrowing all the way to my cliff, boring, banging and blasting (as quietly as they could). At last they had reached my new cellars, and the sight of all the toys together was too much for them: they took all they could. I daresay they were also still angry with the Polar Bear. Also they thought we couldn't get at them.

But I sent my patent green luminous smoke down the tunnel, and Polar Bear blew and blew it with our enormous kitchen bellows. They simply shrieked and rushed out the other (cave) end. But there were Red Gnomes there. I had specially sent for them – a few of the real old families are still in Norway. They captured hundreds of Goblins, and chased many more out into the snow (which they hate). We made them show us where they had hidden things, or bring them all back again, and by Monday we had got practically everything back. The Gnomes are still dealing with the Goblins, and promise there won't be one left by New Year – but I am not so sure – they will crop up again in a century or so, I expect.

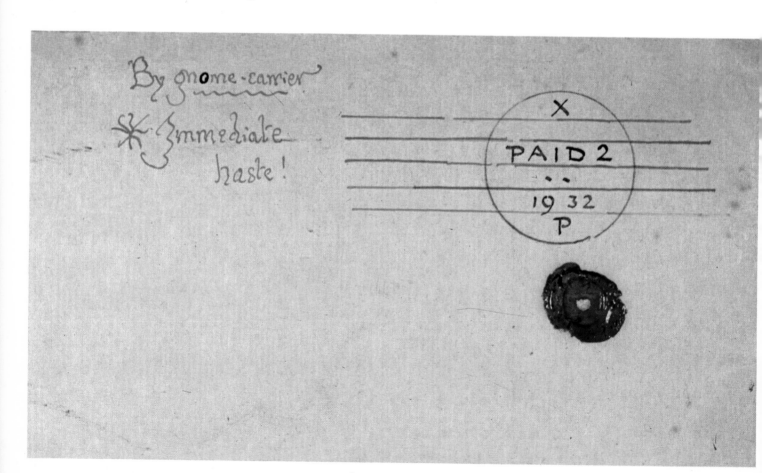

1933

Another Christmas! And I almost thought at one time (in November) that there would not be one this year. There would be the 25th of December of course, but nothing from your old great-great-great-etc. grandfather at the North Pole. My pictures tell you part of the story. *Goblins.* The worst attack we have had for *centuries.* They have been fearfully wild and angry ever since we took all their stolen toys off them last year, and dosed them with green smoke. You remember the Red Gnomes promised to clear all of them out. There was not one to be found in any hole or cave by New Year's Day. But I said they would crop up again – in a century or so. They have not waited so long! They must have gathered their nasty friends from mountains all over the world, and been busy all the summer while we were at our sleepiest. This time we had very little warning. Soon after All Saints' Day, Polar Bear got very restless. He now says he smelt nasty smells – but as usual he did not say anything: he says he did not want to trouble me. He really is a nice old thing, and this time he absolutely saved Christmas. He took to sleeping in the kitchen with his nose towards the cellar-door, opening on the main stairway down into my big stores.

One night, just about Christopher's birthday,* I woke up suddenly. There was squeaking and spluttering in the room and a nasty smell – in my own best green and purple room that I had just had done up most beautifully. I caught sight of a wicked little face at the window. Then I really was upset, for my window is high up above the cliff, and that meant there were bat-riding Goblins about – which we haven't seen since the goblin-war in 1453 that I told you about. I was only just quite awake when a terrific din began far downstairs – in the store-cellars. It would take too long to describe, so I have tried to draw a picture of what I saw when I got down – after treading on a Goblin on the mat. [ONLY THER WAS MORE LIKE 1000 GOBLINS THAN 15. P.B.] (But you could hardly expect me to draw 1000.) Polar Bear was squeezing, squashing, trampling, boxing, and kicking Goblins sky-high, and roaring like a zoo, and the Goblins were yelling like engine whistles. He was splendid. [SAY NO MORE: I ENJOYED IT IMMENSELY!] Well, it is a long story. The trouble lasted for over a fortnight, and it began to look as if I should never be able to get my sleigh out this year. The Goblins had set part of the stores on fire and captured several Gnomes who sleep down there on guard before Polar Bear and some more Gnomes came in – and killed 100 before I arrived. Even when we had put the fire out and cleared the cellars and house (I can't think what they were doing in my room unless they were trying to set fire to my bed) the trouble went on. The ground was black with Goblins under the moon when we looked out, and they had broken up my stables and gone off with

* 21 November

reindeer. I summoned help; there were several battles (every night they used to attack and set fire to the stores) before we got the upper hand, and I am afraid quite a lot of my dear Elves got hurt. Fortunately we have not lost much except my best string (gold and silver) and packing-papers and holly-boxes. I am very short of these: and I have been very short of messengers. Lots of my people are still away (I hope they will come back safe) chasing the Goblins out of my land, those that are left alive. They have rescued all my reindeer. We are quite happy and settled again now, and feel much safer. It really will be centuries before we get another Goblin-trouble. Thanks to Polar Bear and the Gnomes, there can't be very many left at all. [AND FR. C. I WISH I COULD DRAW OR HAD TIME TO TRY – YOU HAVE NO IDEA WHAT THE OLD MAN CAN DOO! LITENING AND FIERWORKS AND THUNDER OF GUNS!] Polar Bear certainly has been busy, helping double help – but he has mixed up some of the girls' presents with the boys' in his hurry. We hope we have got all sorted out – but if you hear of anyone getting a doll when they wanted an engine, you will know why. Actually Polar Bear tells me I am wrong – we did lose a lot of railway stuff – Goblins always go for that – and what we got back was damaged and will have to be repainted. It will be a busy summer next year.

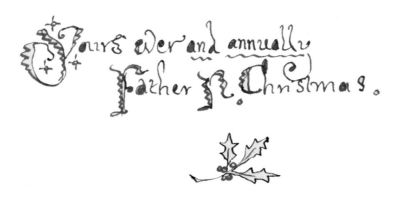

Yours ever and annually
Father N. Christmas.

1934

Very little news. After the frightful business of last year there has not been even a smell of Goblin for 200 miles round. But as I said it would, it took us far into the summer to repair all the damage, and we lost a lot of sleep and rest. When November came round we did not feel like getting to work, and we were rather slow and so have been rushed at the end. Also it has been unusually warm for the North Pole, and Polar Bear still keeps on yawning.

Paksu and Valkotukka have been here a long while. They have grown a good deal – but still get up to frightful mischief in between times of trying to help. This year they stole my paints and painted scrawls on the white walls of the cellars; ate all the mincemeat out of the pies made ready for Christmas; only yesterday went and unpacked half the parcels to find railway things to play with! They don't get on with the Cave-cubs, somehow; several of these have arrived today and are staying here a few nights with old Cave-Bear who is their uncle, grand-uncle, grandfather, great-grand-uncle, etc. Paksu is always kicking them because they squeak and grunt so funnily. Polar Bear has to box him often – and a box from Polar Bear is no joke. As there are no Goblins about and as there is no wind, and so far much less snow than usual, we are going to have a great Boxing Day party ourselves – out-of-doors. I shall ask 100 Elves and Red Gnomes, lots of Polar Cubs, Cave-cubs, and Snow-babies, and of course Paksu and Valkotukka, and Polar Bear, and Cave-Bear and his nephews (etc.) will be there. We have brought a tree all the way from Norway and planted it in a pool of ice. My picture gives you no idea of its size, or of the loveliness of its magic lights of different colours. We tried them yesterday evening to see if they were all right – see picture. If you see a bright glow in the North, you will know what it is. The tree-ish things behind are snowplants, and piled masses of snow made into ornamental shapes – they are purple and black because of darkness and shadow. The coloured things in front are a special edging to the ice-pool – and it is made of real coloured icing. Paksu and Valkotukka are already nibbling at it, though they should not – till the party.

Christmas 1934

1935

No INK this year, and no water, so no painted pictures; also very cold hands, so very wobbly writing. This year it is frightfully cold – snow, snow, snow, and ice. We have been simply buried, messengers have got lost, and found themselves in Nova Scotia, if you know where that is, instead of in Scotland; and Polar Bear could not get home.

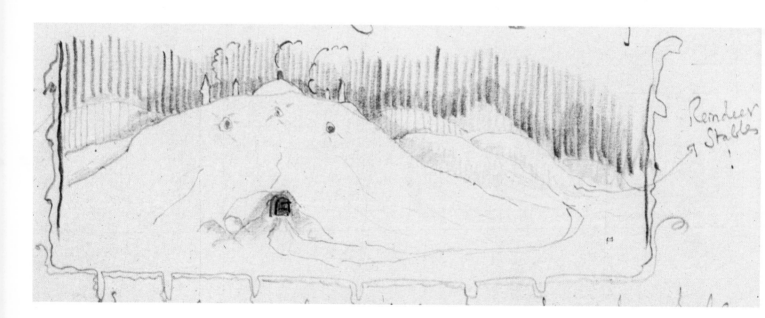

This is a picture of my house about a week ago before we got the reindeer sheds dug out. You can see the tunnel we had to make to the front door. There are only three windows upstairs shining through holes, but you can see steam where the snow is melting off the dome and roof.

Even Polar Bear had to wear a sheepskin coat and red gloves for his paws.

I have had to have a lot of Red Elves to help me. They are very nice and great fun; but although they are very quick they don't get on fast, for they turn everything into a game. Even digging snow.

Polar Bear says that we have not seen the last of the Goblins – in spite of the battles in 1933. They won't dare to come into my land yet; but for some reason they are breeding again and multiplying all over the world. Quite a nasty outbreak. But there are not so many in England, he says. I expect I shall have trouble with them soon. I have given my Elves some new magic sparkler spears that will scare them out of their wits.

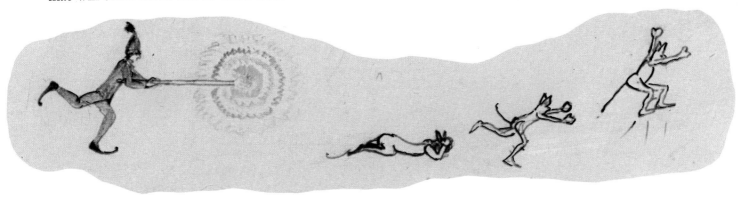

1936

I am sorry I cannot send you a long letter to thank you for yours, but I am sending you a picture which will explain a good deal. I do hope you will like what I am bringing and will forgive any mistakes, and I hope nothing will still be wet! I am still so shaky and upset, I am getting one of my Elves to write a bit more about things:

* * * * *

I am Ilbereth. A lot of us, Red and Green Elves, have gone to live permanently at Cliff House and be trained in the packing business. It was Polar Bear's idea. He said, 'I am going to have a record year and help Father Christmas to get so forward we can have some fun ourselves on Christmas Day.' We all worked hard and you will be surprised to hear that every single parcel was packed and numbered by Saturday last (December 19). Then Polar Bear said, 'I am tired out: I am going to have a hot bath, and go to bed early.' Well, you can see what happened. Father Christmas was taking a last look round in the English Delivery Room about 10 o'clock when water poured through the ceiling and swamped everything: it was soon six inches deep on the floor. Polar Bear had simply got into the bath with both taps running and gone fast asleep with one hind paw on the overflow. He had been asleep two hours when we woke him. Father Christmas was really angry. *But Polar Bear only said, 'I did have a jolly dream. I dreamt I was diving off a melting iceberg and chasing seals.' That made Father Christmas angrier, and Polar Bear said, 'Well, draw a picture of it and ask those children if it is funny or not.' So Father Christmas has. But he has begun to think it funny (although very annoying) himself, now we have cleared up the mess, and got the English presents repacked again. Just in time.*

Best
Wishes
for

1
9
3
7

from

F.C
&
P.B
?

Xtmas 1936 . . F. C.

TIMES

560,783
560,784

A·Merry·Christmas

1937

I am afraid I have not had any time to draw you a picture this year. You see I strained my hand moving heavy boxes in the cellars in November and could not start my letters until later than usual and my hand still gets tired quickly. But Ilbereth, who is now my secretary, has done you what he calls a picture diary. I hope it will do.

*　*　*　*　*

Dear children,

Shall I tell you about my pictures? Polar Bear and Valkotukka and Paksu are always lazy after Christmas, or rather after the St Stephen's Day Party. Father Christmas is ringing for breakfast in vain. Another day when Polar Bear as usual was late, Paksu threw a bath-sponge full of icy water on his face. Polar Bear chased him all round the house and round the garden and then forgave him, because he had not caught Paksu, but had found a huge appetite. We had terrible weather at the end of winter, and actually had rain. *We could not go out for days. I have drawn Polar Bear and his nephews when they did venture out. Paksu and Valkotukka have never gone away. They like it so much that they have begged to stay. It was much too warm at the North Pole this year. A large lake formed at the bottom of the cliff, and left the North Pole standing on an island. I have drawn a view looking* South *so the cliff is on the other side. It was about midsummer. The North Polar Bear took to trying to paddle a boat or canoe, but he fell in so often that the seals thought he liked it, and used to get under the boat and tip it up. That made him annoyed. The sport did not last long as the water froze again early in August. Then we began to begin to think of this Christmas. In my picture, Father Christmas is dividing up the lists and giving me my special lot – you are in it. North Polar Bear of course always pretends to be managing everything: that is why he is pointing, but I am really listening to Father Christmas and I am saluting him, not North Polar Bear.*

We had a glorious bonfire and fireworks to celebrate the Coming of Winter, and the beginning of real 'Preparations'. The snow came down very thick in November and the Elves and Snow-boys had several tobogganing half-holidays. The Polar Cubs were not good

A diary of 1936 to 1937 by Ilbereth

Nobody wants breakfast *after* Christmas. NPB, P. and V are tired 1936. (and full).

A sponge is useful for waking up NPB, but makes him angry.

Late Spring 1937. Thaw and rain. Going for a nice walk to find a lost appetite.

Midsummer. Great hole appears in ice. Seals come out. NPB takes to boating.

Beginning to think of next Christmas. Ilbereth getting orders from F.C.

Celebrating the Coming of Winter. Bonfire party and fireworks.

Tobogganing down from Cliff House. Snowboys have a good time.

Today. Dec. 23rd. NPB busy with the tree — before the disaster.

Tomorrow. Starting with the first load.

A Merry Christmas 1937

F.C.

at it. They fell off, and most of them took to rolling or sliding down just on themselves. Today – but this is the best bit: I had just finished my picture, or I might have drawn it differently. Polar Bear was being allowed to decorate a big tree in the garden, all by himself and a ladder. Suddenly we heard terrible growly-squealy noises. We rushed out to find Polar Bear hanging in the tree himself! 'You are not a decoration,' said Father Christmas. 'Anyway, I am alight,' he shouted. He was. We threw a bucket of water over him, which spoilt a lot of the decorations, but saved his fur. The silly old thing had rested the ladder against a branch (instead of the trunk of the tree). Then he thought, 'I will just light the candles to see if they are working,' although he was told not to. So he climbed to the tip of the ladder with a taper. Just then the branch cracked, the ladder slipped on the snow, and Polar Bear fell into the tree and caught on some wire, and his fur got caught on fire. Luckily he was rather damp, or he might have fizzled. I wonder if roast Polar is good to eat? The last picture is imaginary, and not very good. But I hope it will come true. It will if Polar Bear behaves. I hope you can read my writing. I try to write like dear old Father Christmas (without the trembles), but I cannot do so well. I can write Elvish better:

That is some – but Father Christmas says I write even that too spidery and you would never read it; it says: A very merry Christmas to you all. Love, Ilbereth.

1938

You all will wonder what's the news;
if all has gone well, and if not, who's
to blame; and whether Polar Bear
has earned a mark good, bad, or fair,
for his behaviour since last winter.
Well, first he trod upon a splinter*
and went on crutches in November;
and then one cold day in December
he burnt his nose and singed his paws
upon the kitchen grate, because
without the help of tongs he tried
to roast hot chestnuts. 'Wow!' he cried,
and used a pound of butter (best)
to cure the burns. He would not rest,
but on the twenty-third he went
and climbed up on the roof. He meant
to clear the snow away that choked
his chimney up – of course he poked
his legs right through the tiles, and snow
in tons fell on his bed below.
He has broken saucers, cups and plates;
and eaten lots of chocolates;
he's dropped large boxes on my toes,
and trodden tin soldiers flat in rows;
he's over-wound engines and broken springs,
and mixed up different children's things;
he's thumbed new books and burst balloons
and scribbled lots of smudgy Runes
on my best paper, and wiped his feet

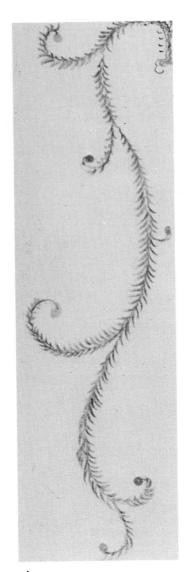

* JUST RHIMING NONSENS: IT WAS A NAIL – RUSTY, TOO! P.B.

on scarves and hankies folded neat –
And yet he has been, on the whole,
a very kind and willing soul.

He's fetched and carried, counted, packed,
and for a week has never slacked:
he's climbed the cellar-stairs at least
five thousand times – the Dear Old Beast!
Paksu sends love, and Valkotukka.
They are still with me; they don't look a
year older, but they're just a bit
more wise, and have a pinch more wit.
The GOBLINS, you'll be glad to hear
have not been seen at all this year,
not near the Pole. But I am told,
they're moving *south,* and getting bold,
and coming back to many lands,
and making with their wicked hands
new mines and caves. But do not fear!
They'll hide away when I appear.

CHRISTMAS DAY: POSTSCRIPT BY ILBERETH

Now Christmas day has come round again –
and poor Polar Bear has got a bad pain!
They say he's swallowed a couple of pounds
of nuts without cracking the shells! It sounds
a Polarish sort of thing to do –
but that isn't all, between me and you:
he's eaten a ton of various goods
and recklessly mixed all his favourite foods,
honey with ham, and turkey and treacle,
and pickles with milk. I think that a week'll
be needed to put the old bear on his feet.
And I mustn't forget his particular treat:
plum pudding with sausages and turkish delight
covered with cream and devoured at a bite!
And after this dish, he stood on his head –
it's rather a wonder the poor fellow's not dead!

ABSOLUTE ROT:
I HAVE *NOT* GOT
A PAIN IN MY POT.
I DO *NOT* EAT
TURKEY OR MEAT:
I STICK TO THE SWEET.
WHICH IS WHY
(AS ALL KNOW) I
AM SO SWEET MYSELF
YOU THINNUOUS ELF!
    GOODBY!

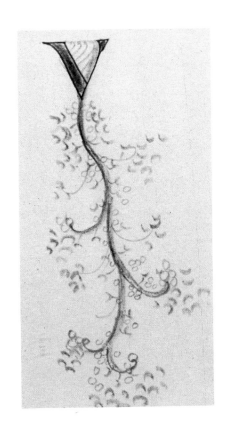

You know my friends too well to think
(although they're rather rude with ink)
that there are really quarrels here!
We've had a very jolly year
(except for Polar's rusty nail):
but now this rhyme must catch the Mail –
a special messenger must go,
in spite of thickly falling snow,
or else this won't get down to you
on Christmas day. It's half past two!
We've quite a ton of crackers still
to pull, and glasses still to fill!
Our love to you on this Noël –
and till the next one, fare you well!

SETTING OUT.

LAST LETTER

I am so glad you did not forget to write to me again this year. The number of children who keep up with me seems to be getting smaller. I expect it is because of this horrible war, and that when it is over things will improve again, and I shall be as busy as ever. But at present so terribly many people have lost their homes, or have left them; half the world seems in the wrong place! And even up here we have been having troubles. I don't mean only with my stores; of course they are getting low. They were already last year, and I have not been able to fill them up, so that I have now to send what I can, instead of what is asked for. But worse than that has happened.

I expect you remember that some years ago we had trouble with the Goblins, and we thought we had settled it. Well it broke out again this autumn, worse than it has been for centuries. We have had several *battles,* and for a while my house was besieged. In November it began to look likely that it would be captured, and all my goods, and that Christmas stockings would remain empty all over the world. Would not that have been a calamity? It has not happened – and that is largely due to the efforts of Polar Bear – but it was not until the beginning of this month that I was able to send out any messengers! I expect the Goblins thought that with so much war going on this was a fine chance to recapture the North. They must have been preparing for some years; and they made a huge new tunnel which had an outlet many miles away. It was early in October that they suddenly came out in *thousands.* Polar Bear says there were at least a *million,* but that is his favourite big number. Anyway he was still fast asleep at the time, and I was rather drowsy myself.

The weather was rather warm for the time of the year, and Christmas seemed far away. There were only one or two Elves about the place; and of course Paksu and Valkotukka (also fast asleep). Luckily Goblins cannot help yelling and beating on drums when they mean to fight; so we all woke up in time, and got the gates and doors barred and the windows shuttered. Polar Bear got on the roof and fired rockets into the Goblin hosts as they poured up the long reindeer-drive; but that did not stop them for long. We were soon surrounded. I have not time to tell you all the story. I had to blow three blasts on the great Horn (Windbeam). It hangs over the fire-place in the hall, and if I have not told you about it before it is because I have not had to blow it for over four hundred years. Its sound carries as far as the North Wind blows. All the same, it was three whole days before help came: Snow-boys, Polar Bears, and hundreds and hundreds of Elves. They came up behind the Goblins; and Polar Bear (really awake this time) rushed out with a blazing branch off the fire in each paw. He must have killed dozens of Goblins (he says a million). But there was a big battle down in the plain near the North Pole in November, in which the Goblins brought hundreds of new companies out of their tunnels. We were driven back to the Cliff, and it was not until Polar Bear and a party of his younger relatives crept out by night, and blew up the entrance to the new tunnels with nearly 100 lbs. of gunpowder, that we got the better of them – for the present. But bang went all the stuff for making fireworks and crackers (the cracking part) for some years. The North Pole cracked and fell over (for the second time) and we have not yet had time to mend it. Polar Bear is rather a hero (I hope he does not think so himself). But of course he is a very MAGICAL animal really, and Goblins can't do much to him, when he is awake and angry. I have seen their arrows bouncing off him and breaking.

Well, that will give you some idea of events, and you will understand why I have not had time to draw a picture this year – rather a pity, because there have been such exciting things to draw – and why I have not been able to collect the usual things for you, or even the very few that you asked for . . .

I suppose after this year you will not be hanging your stocking any more. I shall have to say 'goodbye', more or less: I mean, I shall not forget you. We always keep the names of our old friends, and their letters; and later on we hope to come back when they are grown up and have houses of their own and children . . .

Father Christmas

APPENDIX

Very occasionally the Polar Bear sent a short letter himself. On one occasion he revealed that his true name was Karhu; and he excused his bad English spelling from the fact that the language spoken at the North Pole was *Arctic*. As an example of the language he wrote the sentence *Mára mesta an ni véla tye ento, ya rato nea,* and translated it 'Goodbye till I see you next, and I hope it will be soon.'

After his adventure in the caves, Karhu invented an alphabet from the Goblin marks on the walls, and sent a short letter in it; subsequently, after requests from the children, he sent them the alphabet. Here are both the alphabet and the letter.

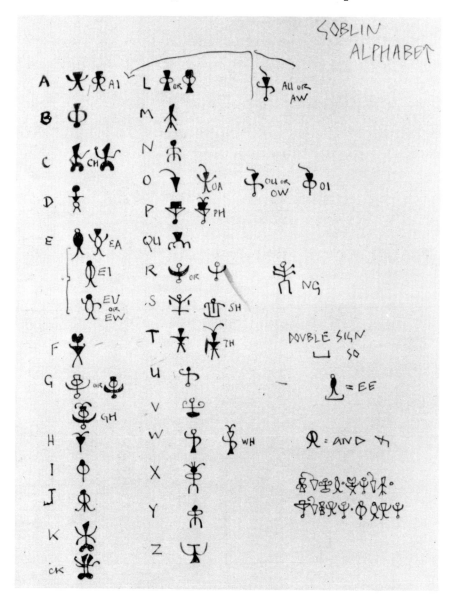

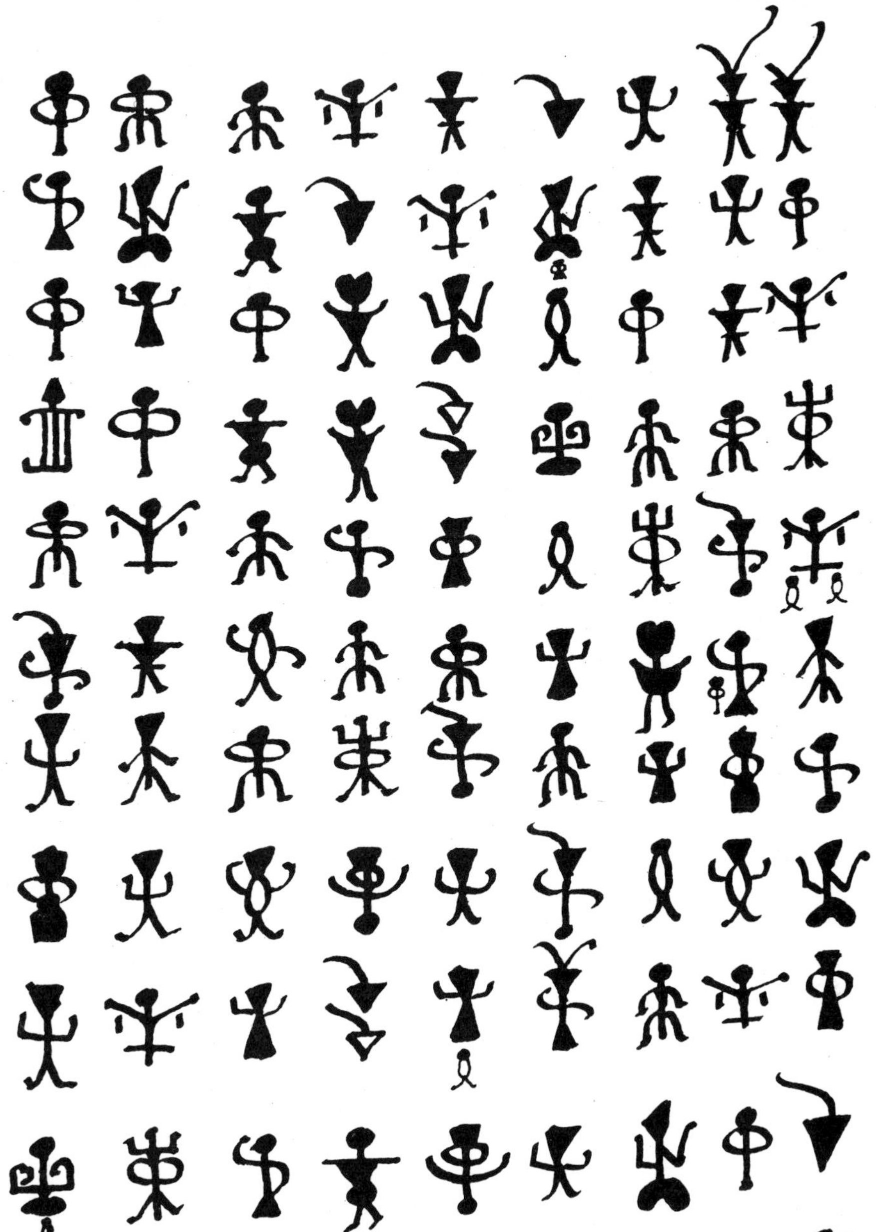

ISBN 0 04 823130 4

Printed in Great Britain
by Westerham Press